HUBBLE BUBBLE
The SUPER-SPOOKY FRIGHT NIGHT!

TRACEY CORDEROY

illustrated by JOE BERGER

An imprint of Candlewick Press

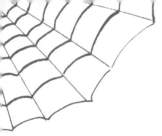

First U.S. hardcover edition 2017

Library of Congress Catalog Card Number 2015938143
ISBN 978-0-7636-8653-6 (paperback)
ISBN 978-0-7636-9502-6 (hardcover)

17 18 19 20 21 22 BVG 10 9 8 7 6 5 4 3 2 1

Printed in Berryville, VA, U.S.A.

This book was typeset in Baskerville MT.
The illustrations were done in pen and ink and digitally.

Nosy Crow
an imprint of
Candlewick Press
99 Dover Street
Somerville, Massachusetts 02144

www.nosycrow.com
www.candlewick.com

For Anna,
with love x
T. C.

For Mum and Dad,
with love x
J. B.

CONTENTS

The
Super-Spooky
FRIGHT NIGHT!

Chapter One

"Pumpkin pop!" cried Granny Crow.

"Lemon soda!" said Granny Podmore.

They turned to Pandora. "Which drink would you prefer, dear?"

Pandora and her friends were getting things ready for a Halloween party at Pandora's house. But Pandora's two grandmothers couldn't agree on a *thing*.

Granny P. was neat and sensible. But Granny C. was (*whisper it!*) a witch, so sometimes *her* ideas were just a bit . . . different.

"Pumpkin pop!" said Pandora's friends, giggling. Bluebell, Nellie, Clover, and Jake liked Pandora's witchy grandmother very

much. Once her pet frog had magicked their teacher's clothes away, leaving him in just his underwear!

"Or we could have both?" suggested Pandora, as Granny Podmore now looked disappointed.

"Perfect!" cried the grandmothers, and they got to work.

Granny Podmore filled a jug with watery lemon soda while Granny Crow fired up her cauldron and started to toss in ingredients . . .

"Thirteen tiny pumpkins . . . ten pints of stuff-and-nonsense . . . and a good-sized squirt of popping juice. There!" She smiled.

While the potion brewed, Pandora and
her friends made spooky decorations.
Nellie draped sheets over tables and chairs
to make them look like ghosts, Pandora
made pom-pom spiders, Clover
did pipe-cleaner snakes, and

Bluebell and Jake turned an
old cardboard box into a
fantastic spooky castle!

As they worked, Granny Podmore flitted around, flicking her duster at anything that got too messy, while humming happy tunes with Granny Crow.

That's better, thought Pandora. She liked it when her grandmothers got along.

In no time at all Pandora's living room looked like a haunted wood. And Pandora, being a witch like Granny Crow, *loved* it!

"Oh, but I wish we had glitter," said Pandora, "to sprinkle on the castle, like frost."

"Here—I'll do it!" chirped Granny Crow. She waved her wand, and pot after pot of sparkly glitter appeared.

"Hooray!" cheered the children, grabbing the pots and glittering everything in sight.

"Oh, but the MESS!" gasped Granny Podmore. This called for emergency action!

Scurrying to the cupboard, back she came with her super-sucky vacuum. It looked like an octopus with a big smiley face, and its tentacles were tubes with brushes and nozzles on the ends.

"Lucky I brought Ollie!" Granny Podmore nodded. She aimed a tentacle at the floor and . . .

SUCK!

Suddenly all the glitter on the carpet vanished, along with some small scraps of paper and pipe cleaners.

"Oh, but I love a little glitter on *my* carpet," Granny Crow piped up, looking puzzled.

Then Granny Podmore went too far. SUCK! A spider on Granny C.'s hat went whooshing up one of Ollie's tentacles.

Granny Crow frowned.

"Give Sam back right now!"

When Sam, the pet spider, was back in place, it was time to start on the party food.

Granny Podmore baked her special gingerbread men and made some yummy (and very neat) sandwiches. Granny Crow, however, followed only *magical* recipes . . .

With a flick of her wand, jars and bottles appeared in ALL shapes and sizes. One bottle looked like a crescent moon and was filled with a bright silver powder. The label said Moonlight.

"*Wow*," gasped Clover.

A star-shaped jar had fluffy balls inside that floated around like dandelion clocks.

"Those are fairy wishes," Granny Crow said. "Whatever you make with them tastes like whatever you wish it to!"

Smiling, she opened her magical cookbook and helped the children with the recipes.

With just two *tiny* sprinkles of Moonlight
their grape jelly turned from purple to silver
and sparkled like the shiniest moon!

Then they spooned the batter into the tin
and put a fairy wish in every one.

When they were baked, Jake tested one

to see if you *really* tasted what you wished
for . . .

"Yep!" He grinned, licking his lips.
"Burger and fries!"

When the last tray was in the oven,
Granny Podmore and Pandora went into
the living room to make some decorations
for the party table.

Granny Podmore folded some plain white napkins into the *neatest* swans. Then they made some terrifically tidy paper chains.

"Let's show the others!" said Pandora, beaming. But back in the kitchen, things weren't quite so spick-and-span.

Granny C. had been making some "little extras," and the place was now splattered! Her food might be magical, but boy— what a messy chef!

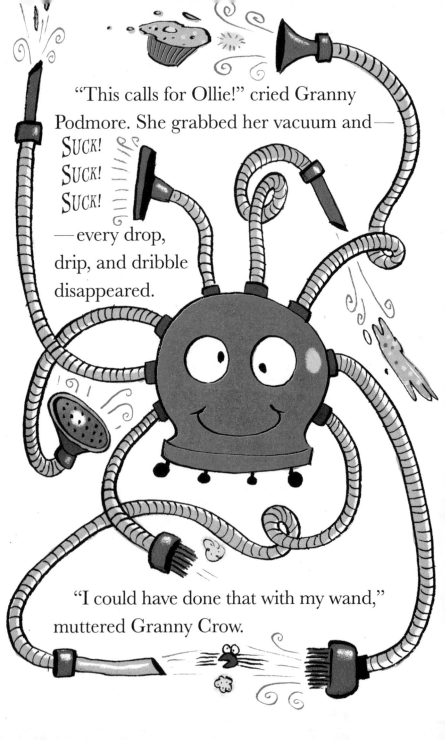

"This calls for Ollie!" cried Granny Podmore. She grabbed her vacuum and—

SUCK!
SUCK!
SUCK!

—every drop, drip, and dribble disappeared.

"I could have done that with my wand," muttered Granny Crow.

Now everyone took the
delicious food to the party table.

"Neat swans!" said Bluebell.

"Thank you!" said Granny Podmore.

Granny Crow's food looked wonderful,
too. There were bat-shaped cookies that
hung around the bowls, and a custard
cat (that actually meowed!). There were
chocolate-roll snail cakes, broomstick chips
that really flew, and bright orange pumpkin
pop simmered in Granny Crow's cauldron.

The party was due to start any minute: as soon as more friends arrived!

"Oh, but we haven't got *costumes*!" Pandora gasped.

She and Granny Crow waved their wands together, and everyone found themselves dressed up.

Jake was a vampire bat, Nellie was a witch, Pandora was a spider, Bluebell was a ghost, and Clover was a fluffy little werewolf.

"I-I don't need a costume!" Granny Podmore quickly said. Costumes could be so messy.

"Oh, but I have the *perfect* one for you," said Granny Crow with a smile.

With a flick of her wand, Granny Podmore's plain dress became a magnificent peacock outfit.

"And look!" Granny P. smiled, suddenly noticing that the tail was made out of feather dusters. Now she could dust lots of things at the same time!

DING DONG! went the doorbell. It was
party time! Pandora dashed over and
opened the door, and an excited crowd
hurried in.

There were mummies and monsters.
There were witches and wizards. There
were cats — and bats — and rats!

"Oooh!" gasped everyone when they saw
the decorations. *"Wicked!"*

"Time for some party games!"
Pandora cried.

"Musical chairs?"
suggested Granny
Podmore.

"No—musical
broomsticks!" cried
Granny Crow.

When she swished her wand, a pile of broomsticks appeared, along with some flapping paper bats.

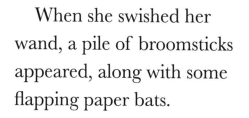

Then
the piano
started playing a
spooky tune.

"It's the **Fright Night Party Mix**!" Pandora smiled. "My favorite!"

Granny Crow gathered the children together. "Take a broomstick each and fly around," she said, "and when the music stops, catch as many paper bats as you can!"

Cheering, the children climbed onto their broomsticks and zoomed up into the air.

"Yay!" they giggled
as broomsticks bashed and
paper bats zipped around like
rockets. And when stray broom twigs
rained onto the carpet,
Granny P. was there to
sweep them up
with her tail feathers!

Finally Bluebell won the game
and got a chocolate broomstick
medal. But Granny Crow had
lots more magical games up
her sleeve.

Next they played Pin-the-Tail-on-the-Werewolf, then Sleeping Lions (though Granny C. changed it to *roaring* ones instead!), then Leapfrog with real, live frogs, which was fun!

It was all going well. *So* well. Granny Crow was a party sensation! But *then* she went to check on her pumpkin pop . . .

"Oh," sighed Granny, peering into the cauldron. "I don't think it's poppy enough."

Pandora looked at her nervously. She really hoped Granny wouldn't spoil things by going too far . . .

"I think it's fine!" Pandora gulped.

"Ummm . . . no," said Granny. "It needs more oomph! Just one last *teeny-tiny* spell, that's all."

Pandora had a very bad feeling about
this. But before she could stop her,
Granny swished her wand and uttered
the oomph-iest spell she knew . . .

"POPPIOCIOUS!"

In a flash of starry light the cauldron started shaking. Then POP! went the pop.

Super-fizzy potion now blooped over the sides, and small orange pumpkins were popping out everywhere, wearing happy little grins.

"Oh!" Granny Crow jumped in shock, *and her wand tumbled into the cauldron!*

"Don't worry!" she spluttered, as a crowd gathered around. "I'm in control!"

But things had never been more OUT of control. The carpet was disappearing under a sticky orange ocean, and the pumpkins (wound up on super-fizzy pop) were now having a crazy food fight.

"I'll see to this!" said Granny Podmore with a nod.

"No! I can do it!" cried Granny Crow. "Just trust me!"

Chapter Four

Granny Crow fished her drippy wand from the cauldron. "Oh, it *hates* getting wet," she sighed. It was sparking and letting off a low, growly sound like a burp.

But Pandora had other things on her mind. "Granny!" She pointed. "There! Look at the pumpkins!"

The little horrors were now wearing ghost sheets and running around wailing, *"Whoooo!"*

Problem was, they couldn't see where they were going and were bumping into *everything* . . . *Crash!* The hat stand toppled onto the piano, which made a loud plonk and sent Cobweb, Granny Crow's nervous cat, shooting up a curtain and hissing wildly.

"Yikes!" Pandora gulped, peering around for calm, sensible Granny Podmore. But no! Granny P. had disappeared—*just when they needed her!*

Now a ghost spun around and started to head for Jake and Bluebell's castle. The pesky little pumpkins were going to *ruin* it.

"Eeek!" squeaked Pandora. "Nooooo!"

But then — just in the
nick of time — Granny Podmore
flew past with her super-sucky vacuum.

"Ollie to the rescue!" she yelled with
pride, and . . .

SUUUUUCCCKKKKK!

The gloppy orange ocean disappeared instantly, and all the naughty pumpkins with it.

BA-DOINK! BA-DOINK! BA-DOINK! they went as they bumped along inside Ollie's tentacles, as though they were riding a crazy waterslide!

Plopping into his tummy, they looked *so* mad. The children watched them through a little round window. They were shaking their fists and stomping their little orange feet.

Pandora's eyes widened, but Granny Podmore smiled.

"Don't worry," she said. "They're not hurt in the slightest! And we'll set them free—just not in here. Come with me!"

Everyone followed her into the backyard. Then Granny Podmore flicked a switch and Ollie hiccupped the pumpkins back out. The stompy little things had probably been giving him indigestion!

Before the pumpkins could sneak back into the house, Pandora showed them her trampoline, which they thought was the best thing ever! Still wild from the pop, they bounced up and down like they had ants in their little orange pants.

"WHOOPEE!"

Back inside, everyone started jumping around to the spooky music! Pandora hugged her grandmothers. It was great that they were so different, and both so lovely, too!

"So, who wants some pumpkin pop?" asked Granny Crow. "I think my wand's fixed again!"

Pandora and Granny Podmore laughed.

"Maybe not, Granny," said Pandora. "I think we've had enough excitement for one night!"

And that was one thing both grandmothers *had* to agree on!

TEDDY
TROUBLE!

Chapter One

"I'm making a polar bear!" Nellie said.

"I'm doing a grizzly," said Jake with a grin.

"A panda!" cried Bluebell.

"A ballet bear!" Clover smiled.

"The honey bears look nice," said Pandora.

It was Nellie's birthday, and her party was at the Fluffy Friends store in town. At Fluffy Friends you could make your own teddy bear. You could *even* record a special message to go inside your bear, so when you pressed its tummy it would talk!

Pandora couldn't wait to start making her bear. Although she *did* hope that Granny Crow—who'd come "to help"—

wouldn't get too excited and go too far . . .

"Oooh!" said Granny, smiling at the bears in their snazzy little outfits. "Remember that time," she said to Pandora, "I magicked up a bear in the supermarket, and a *darling* little dragon at your school party when the barbecue wouldn't light?"

Pandora remembered the *dragon*, all right.
Besides the burgers, it had barbecued half
the soccer field!

"Granny," said Pandora nervously,
"um . . . have you brought your *wand*
today?"

"Of course!" said Granny. "I take my
wand everywhere, dear!"

Nodding, Pandora then said in a whisper,
"But Granny, no magic is allowed in this
store. I think those are the rules."

"Don't worry." Granny tittered. "I'm here to help! And a little *helpful* magic never hurt *anyone*."

With that, she hurried everyone along
to pick out the accessories for their bears.

Nellie's mom and two **Fluffy Friends** assistants trailed along behind. The assistants wore badges with their names — Tom P. and Jess.

Pandora thought Jess looked really bored, and Tom P. seemed terrified of Granny. When she asked if they ever made teddy *werewolves,* Tom was off like a shot to "help at the register!"

Along the back wall was a tall stack of shelves filled with accessories for making the bears. Pandora spied the honey-bear things up on the very top shelf. But they looked *way* too high for even the grown-ups to reach.

DRESS YOUR BEAR!

Jess was now checking the messages on her phone, and Tom P. was dusting the cash register. So Pandora asked Nellie's mom if she thought there might be a ladder they could use.

"Oh, but we don't need a *ladder*," said Granny. And out came her wand.

"I can do it!"

Chapter Two

Before Pandora could stop her, Granny wiggled her wand at the shelves.

The problem was, she waved it a little too excitedly, and everything started flying off — little accessories like ballet skirts, swimsuits, explorer clothes, and pajamas! Groaning, Pandora covered her eyes.

"Oh no . . ."

Luckily Jess hadn't seen.

She'd been far too busy texting. As for Tom P., he was too scared to say a word.

Nellie's mom, however, looked a little annoyed. Pandora's mom, Moonbeam, had warned her all about Granny's "magical meddling."

"Pssst — Granny," hissed Pandora. *"Please make that stop!"*

"Um—yes!" blurted Granny, her cheeks turning pink.
"Right away!"

With a flick of her wand, everything was back in order and the children were holding what they needed.

"We're ready!" called Pandora, and Jess looked up.

"OK," she said in a bored voice. "Follow me."

She led them to the Fluffing Machine to fill their bears with fluff.

But when she switched it on, nothing happened.

With a sigh, Jess gave the machine a swift kick. "This is always happening," she said. The machine whirred to life and some lights flashed on.

"OK," yawned Jess. "Fill your bears with fluff until they're soft and cuddly."

"Hooray!" cheered the children, getting into a line by the fluff tube.

Nellie went first. Then Jake. Then Clover. Then Bluebell filled Poppy Panda. Finally, it was Pandora's turn.

"Come on, James!" said Pandora brightly, lifting her honey bear to the fluff tube. But suddenly the machine juddered to a stop. Then fell silent.

"*Ooooohhh,*" groaned Jess, "I'm *sick* of this. Tom P.—the machine's stopped *again.* Come over here and give it a kick."

"C-can't!" spluttered Tom, still eyeing Granny nervously. "I've—um—got a bad foot!"

"*Doh . . .*" said Jess, looking *really* fed up. "*Fine . . .*"

Rolling her eyes, she gave the machine a good hefty kick. But this time nothing happened. Not a thing.

Jess turned to Pandora, who was just behind her, still clutching her floppy teddy.

"Silly machine!" tutted Jess. "This time I think it's broken for good."

"Oh, no!" squeaked Pandora. Her face fell. All her friends' bears were nice and cuddly!

With that, Granny sidled up. "Don't worry," she whispered, sneaking out her wand. "You'll soon have a fluffy friend, too!"

"Thanks, Granny," Pandora whispered back. "You're the best!"

Chapter Three

Granny gave her wand a short, sharp flick, and the Fluffing Machine whirred back to life.

"Oh!" said Pandora, trying to sound surprised. Luckily she'd been the only one who'd seen Granny do the spell.

"What's going on?" muttered Jess. The machine sounded healthier than ever.

"Er," said Pandora, quickly filling James with fluff. "Your kicking must be better than you thought!"

Nellie's mom, however, didn't seem to think so. With narrowed eyes, she looked Granny up and down. But Granny had already slipped her wand away and was whistling innocently.

"Thanks, Granny," said Pandora under her breath, cuddling a beautifully plump James. "But please — *no more magic!* OK?"

After that, Granny was on her *best* behavior. She sat nicely when the children recorded messages to go inside their bears. She sat nicely when the talk buttons were popped in their tummies and the teddies gently sewn up. And she sat *so* nicely when the children chose spare outfits for their bears.

Only once did she get a *little* carried away and magically changed James's overalls into a wickedly wild *werewolf* suit. But she changed them back as soon as Pandora complained.

Now it was time to make the bears *talk* by pressing the talk button in their tummies . . .

"Watch me dance!" squealed Clover's little ballet bear.

"Grrrr!" Jake's grizzly growled.

"Poppy Panda loves Bluebell!" Bluebell's panda said brightly.

"Happy Birthday!" cried Nellie's polar bear.

And James, Pandora's honey bear, called, *"Time for some honey!"*

The children loved making their bears talk and pressed their tummies *all the time*.

But, after a while, Pandora noticed that something was wrong with James. The more she pressed his tummy, the slower he spoke . . .

Press!

"Time fooor some honeey!"

Press!

"Tiiimmee foooooorrr sooome honeeey."

Press!

"Tiiiiiiimmmmmmmmmmmeeeeee fooooooooooorrrrrrrrrrrrrrr soooooome honeeeeeey."

Upset, Pandora plodded over to Granny and explained that James was broken.

"Oh dear!" said Granny. "Here, let's see."

Taking James, she pressed his tummy gently. But now he wasn't talking at all.

"Don't worry," whispered Granny. "I can sort him out. But I *will* have to use my wand . . ."

Pandora nodded. It was the only way.

Granny took out her wand and was tapping James's tummy when Nellie skipped over with *her* bear.

"What's your grandmother doing?" she asked.

"Fixing James," Pandora whispered.

"Here!" said Granny, handing him back. "Try now."

Carefully, Pandora pressed James's tummy and . . .

"Phew, that's better!" he said.

"What?" gasped Pandora.

"I can talk again!" James giggled. *"Thanks, Granny!"*

Pandora could hardly believe her ears. Her teddy was really talking!

Nellie instantly turned to Granny, her eyes big and bright. "Can you make *my* bear do that too, *please* . . . ?"

Chapter
Four

Granny (always happy to have a chance
to do magic!) made Nellie's teddy talk
too. Pandora began to feel worried again.
Granny was getting excited, and that
spelled trouble . . .

"*Hi, Nellie!*" the little polar bear said.
"*By the way, what's my name?*"

"Um—Sophie, I think!" Nellie smiled.

"*Good choice!*" Sophie giggled.

Nellie clapped her hands. A talking bear was the best birthday present ever! But— not only could the two bears *talk*—now it seemed they could *walk* too!

James jumped to his feet and bounded off. *"Sophie, let's play chase!"*

"Hooray!" cheered Sophie, racing behind. *"Coming!"*

Now *all* the children wanted their
bears to "do stuff," and before Nellie's
mom could open her mouth, Granny had
brought them all to life.

In a blink they were all racing around,
which Pandora felt *sure* wasn't allowed.

"*Oh, Granny . . .*" she said.

"What?" Granny grinned. "They're only having fun!"

Jess looked dumbstruck, Tom P. looked terrified, and Nellie's mom gasped in horror. Pandora and her friends tried to round up the bears. But the teddies were fast. And Poppy Panda was a real trouble-maker!

Making a beeline for the machines, she pressed *all* the buttons, flicked *all* the switches, and swung on *any* lever she could reach.

With a rumbly whir, the machines sprang to life and started going crazy.

"I don't think they like all their switches flipped at once!" said Pandora.

The **Happy Faces Machine** started shooting out bear noses. The **Chatterbox Machine** began coughing out talk buttons. And the sewing machines started stitching bear outfits double quick!

But the **Fluffing Machine** went the craziest of all. Soon it was burping out huge dollops of white fluff.

"It's snowing!" Poppy giggled, catching huge pawfuls. Pandora and her friends raced over to Granny.

"Can you round up the bears?" Bluebell asked.

"Of course!" Granny smiled.

"Please do, then!" grumbled Nellie's mom. "And while you're at it, turn them all back to normal!"

The teddies were now huddled in a corner, whispering. Pandora felt sure they were up to something.

Granny slipped out her wand. But before she could wave it, the bears suddenly broke apart.

Now clutched very tightly in James's fluffy paws was Nellie's mom's basket. Inside it was lunch for Nellie's birthday party. *Uh-oh* . . .

"Hey, come back!" Nellie cried as the teddies bounded over to the open window and, one by one, flew through it, giggling.

"Really!" spluttered Nellie's mom. "How very rude!"

Everyone hurried out into the street, but the teddies had disappeared. Then . . .

"Look!" cried Pandora, pointing at the
pavement. "A clue!"

The teddies had left a trail of the fluff
that had exploded from the Fluffing
Machine.

"They're playing a 'follow-the-trail' game!" squealed Clover.

"Cool!" cried Jake. "Let's find them!"

The fluff trail led right down the street, then through a gate into the park. At last, the children found the playful little

bears sitting around a picnic blanket with Nellie's party food, all laid out just right.

"*Surprise*," said James, giggling. "*A teddy bears' picnic!*"

Everyone ate snacks and cakes, which tasted so yummy in the sunshine.

"Granny, thanks for *helping*." Pandora grinned. If Granny hadn't made the teddies "do stuff," this treat would never have happened.

"It's my best birthday ever!" Nellie said, beaming.

Granny looked pleased.

"Well, I'm glad," she said. "It's been such a . . . magical day!"

And everyone laughed—except for James, whose mouth was full of honey-crunch cookies.
Yum!

GRANNY MAKES
A SPLASH!

Chapter
One

Pandora's teacher peered out the window
as the bus taking them to the swimming
pool shuddered to a stop.

"What's wrong,
Mr. Bibble?"
asked Pandora
and Nellie,
looking over
the seat.

Their teacher tapped the bus driver, who whispered something back.

"Oh, no!" cried Mr. Bibble. "A flat tire!"

All over the bus, children started to chatter.

"Quiet!" Mrs. Appleton snapped.

Mrs. Appleton was the math teacher.
But on Tuesday afternoons Mr. Grimly
took her class so that she could help with
swimming.

Nobody liked Mrs. Appleton.
She was as round and
sour as a crab apple.

So her nickname was Crabby-Appleton. Crabby for short.

Crabby thumped down the bus aisle, but halfway along she stopped.

Granny C., who had also come to help, suddenly put up her hand.

"Yes?" barked Crabby.

"Well," Granny said, smiling, "I'm a whiz at fixing tires, you know." She whisked out her wand, but Crabby glowered.

"Absolutely not!"

Nose in the air, Crabby marched up to Mr. Bibble. "Well, don't just *sit* there." She scowled at him. "Come and help me fix that tire!"

She turned to the bus driver. "Go and get your tools!"

"But I d-don't have any tools with me," he muttered.

"What?" yelled Crabby sourly. "How ridiculous!"

With that, Granny swept past, her wand high in the air.

"Eeek!" said Pandora. This didn't look good. If Granny did magic after Crabby had said *not* to, there was going to be BIG trouble.

And sure enough . . .

"Look here," said Granny, striding off the bus. "I'll just do a *teeny-weeny* spell to get us to the swimming pool."

The children's noses were now pressed to the windows. What would Granny do?

Crabby marched out, blowing her whistle, but Granny had already waved her wand, and . . .

BANG!

When the magic mist cleared, the bus
was gone and five old-fashioned circus
caravans stood there in its place.

Each one was pulled by a big, friendly horse and held six delighted children. Granny had magicked up jugglers, too. And acrobats.

"There!" said Granny, beaming, as Crabby gaped. "*Horses* don't get flats, do they? Hop in!"

Chapter Two

Crowds of people waved as the circus
headed to the pool. When they got there,
Mr. Bibble hurried everyone inside to
change.

"And no more nonsense from *you*," sniffed
Crabby, as Granny held open the door.

"Nonsense, dear?" said Granny,
surprised. She'd saved the day!

Mr. Bibble took the boys to get changed
while Crabby and Granny took the girls.

But the girls' changing room was a mess. The school before had left dirty laundry and trash all over the floor.

"Don't worry, I'll clean this up!" said Granny.

"No!" Pandora squeaked. But Granny was already muttering a makeover spell . . .

"*Fluffy towels, soft and white. Rainbow showers, sparkly bright. Chandeliers with gems like ice. Fill this room with all things nice!*"

POP!

Now the messy changing room became the fanciest bathroom ever! The showers had gold faucets in the shape of fish, the floor was made of marble, and a crystal chandelier twinkled overhead.

"Wow," gasped the girls. It looked just like a palace!

Everyone skipped away to the showers to wash in rainbow bubbles. Crabby, though, madder than ever, was heading their way . . .

"How many times," she said, glowering at Granny, "must I tell you not to meddle! Now I'm warning you—no more *you-know-what*!"

"You know . . . what?" said Granny, puzzled.

"Magic," whispered Pandora.

Before Crabby could utter another word, Pandora pointed out that it was time for the lesson.

"OK, then, girls," called Crabby, "off we go!"

The pool was amazing—it had waterfalls and slides, and even a wave machine. There was also a huge inflatable iceberg with three blow-up penguins on top.

Pandora's friend Jake had had his
swimming party here,
and it had been
really fun!

But today the iceberg and slides were roped off. The waterfalls were turned off, too.

"Too bad," said Pandora with a sigh.

"Yeah." Nellie nodded.

All they were allowed to do in school lessons was swim back and forth with kickboards. And Pandora's group was taught by Crabby, who stood on the side the whole time, yelling, "Kick harder!"

As the children swam *endlessly* from side to side, Granny had to sit sensibly and be "in charge" of the kickboards.

But the kickboards didn't *need* being "in charge" of. Why *would* they? Kickboards never did anything! So Granny just wriggled, and wiggled, and sighed, and checked the clock as the time ticked on slowly. *Yawn* . . .

And then, just before the end of the lesson—as Granny sat twiddling her thumbs—she had the most wonderful idea.

Checking to see if the coast was clear, she secretly slipped out her wand. It was time to liven things up a bit, *Granny style!*

Chapter Three

"Miss!" Jake suddenly yelled from the water. "That penguin over there just winked!"

He pointed at one of the inflatable penguins.

"Nonsense!" snapped Crabby.

"But Miss—it did!" cried Jake. "I *really* saw it!"

Pandora, who was swimming nearby, looked up *as the penguin winked again!*

"*Uh-oh . . .*" she muttered. This had to be Granny. It *had* to!

While Crabby and Jake argued on, Pandora swam over to Granny.

"Psst, Granny," she whispered up from the water, "did *you* make that penguin wink?"

"I . . . *might* have." Granny grinned.

"OK—I did! I just wanted the last five minutes of your lesson to be fun!"

With that, she flicked her wand again and all three penguins started waddling along their iceberg.

"The penguins! Look—they're moving!" Bluebell squealed.

One by one, the penguins plopped into

the water where Mr. Bibble was blowing
bubbles with his beginners.

"Arrgh!" he spluttered. "W-what's going
on?" But Crabby knew, all right.

"Pandora's grandmother!" she said
angrily. "That's what!"

As Crabby stomped over to Granny,
the penguins in the pool were having a
great time. The more Mr. Bibble shooed
them away, the more they jumped on and
off their iceberg, sending water splashing
everywhere.

"Stop them!" Mr. Bibble called.

"Oh, don't you worry," said Crabby.
"I will!"

As soon as she was close enough, Crabby
snatched the wand from Granny's hand.

"Hey!" Granny frowned. "I'll have you know, wands should be handled with care."

Crabby frowned back. "And I'll have *you* know that magic is not allowed in school swimming lessons!"

Crabby whisked the wand out of Granny's reach. But as she did, a swirl of stars came shooting out of it.

"Oh, *now* look what you've done," groaned Granny.

"What?" Crabby glowered.

"You've just gone and cast a *spell*," said Granny.

Pandora watched the magical stars as they zipped and zoomed through the air. They sparkled like moonlight and looked full of mischief!

A swirl of them swept around the waterfall, and it instantly gushed to life.

Other stars bounced off a long, straight slide, which turned into a giant roller coaster. The inflatable iceberg got zapped by stars, too, and magically grew into a *real* block of shimmering ice!

"Hooray!" cheered the children, splashing away to have fun.

"To the *roller coaster*!" Nellie called.

But Pandora had spotted a bunch of naughty stars bouncing up and down on the diving board. They were getting *wilder* by the second. What next?!

Chapter Four

WHOOSH!

The stars dive-bombed into the water and pinged off the wave machine like hailstones.

With a small spurt of bubbles, the machine blooped to life. Soft, gentle waves began rippling through the pool.

"Yippee!" cheered the children. Waves were great! Too bad Mr. Bibble didn't think so.

"Out of the water, please, children!" he called.

"Oh, but it's fun!" Bluebell cried. Everyone agreed. No *way* were they getting out now!

Soon the children were whizzing down the roller-coaster slide, playing pirates under the waterfalls, and bobbing aound in the soft, bouncy waves like dolphins!

Up on the iceberg, Jake, Clover, and Bluebell had just started a game of Arctic explorers when Nellie and Pandora appeared.

"This is our flag!" Nellie announced, sticking a kickboard into the ice.

Then Pandora declared the new kingdom as their land.

"But *we* got here *first*," Bluebell
said with a frown.

"Ah, but you need a *flag* to make it *yours*!"
Nellie said.

Meanwhile, on the side of the pool, the
grown-ups were arguing, too. Suddenly,
Granny made a grab for her wand, but
Crabby had seen that coming.

"Oh-no-you-don't!" Crabby said,
dodging out of the way. But the floor was
wet and her foot slipped.

"Help!" shrieked Crabby. "I'm falling!"

Crabby grabbed Granny's arm to steady
herself, but *Granny* started wobbling, too.
Then down they both tumbled into the
water . . .

Splash!

"Granny!" gasped Pandora, now
swimming toward them. She could see that
Crabby still had the wand.

But that wasn't *all* she could see . . .

"Giant wave!" yelled Pandora. "Everyone onto the iceberg!"

Squeals of excitement filled the air as the children clambered onto the iceberg, along with three penguins, two drippy teachers, and Granny!

A few moments later the massive wave hit with one huge foamy CRASH!

"Hey — it's giving us a *ride*," said Jake, grinning, as the wave nosed their iceberg out of the pool . . . then out the door . . . *then along the busy streets.*

"Beep, beep!" cried Pandora as traffic swerved out of the way.

At last, the iceberg slid to a stop in the middle of Pandora's school playground. It had brought them *all* the way back—and what a ride!

Jumping off, the children started skipping around it.

"Hooray for our ice bus!" they cried.

Granny got off next, followed by Crabby. Her face was a seasick-y shade of green, and she *still* held Granny's wand.

"Thank you!" Granny said, grabbing it and stuffing it into her pocket.

Finally, Mr. Bibble staggered from the iceberg, the very last to leave.

Or *was* he . . . ?

"Look!" shouted Pandora as three little penguins came waddling off behind him.

"New school pets! Yippee!" cheered the children.

Granny looked very pleased, too. Fishing in her pocket again, she took out her wand.

"Time to make the school pond just a tiny bit bigger . . ."

The End